I0647310

EDGES

Broken String

Book 5

Bjorn Esterday Was Not Born Yesterday

Wynter Sommers

GJ dePillis

TXu001885818
PAu 3-627-478, 1-798104171, PAu003401882, PAu003759141,
1-787-353831
Library of Congress Control Number: 2019930924

Published by Pure Force Enterprises, Inc.
California, USA
Since 2002

ISBN-13: 978-1-7184-0006-1
ISBN-10: 1-7184-0006-3

DEDICATION

To all of us whose hearts reach out to change the world around, whose minds calculate the next strategic move, whose souls crave adventure and value the freedoms of democracy. To the spirit harnessing the power of fiction to alter our reality, making the world a better place for everyone.

Bjorn Series Alternate Reading Plan

1st	Edges Book 1
2nd	Edges Book 2
3rd	Gone Book 1
4th	Firebrand Book 1
5th	Edges Book 3
6th	Firebrand Book 2
7th	Gone Book 2
8th	Gone Book 3
9th	Firebrand Book 3
10th	Gone Book 4
11th	Firebrand Book 4
12th	Gone Book 5
13th	Gone Book 6
14th	Edges Book 4
15th	Firebrand Book 5
16th	Gone Book 7
17th	Firebrand Book 6
18th	Gone Book 8
19th	Firebrand Book 7
20th	Gone Book 9
21st	Firebrand Book 8
22nd	Gone Book 10
23rd	Gone Book 11
24th	Gone Book 12
25th	Gone Book 13
26th	Firebrand Book 9 (End)
27th	Gone Book 14
28th	Gone Book 15
29th	Gone Book 16
30th	Gone Book 17
31st	Gone Book 18 (End)
32nd	Edges Book 5
33rd	Edges Book 6
34th	Edges Book 7
35th	Edges Book 8
36th	Edges Book 9 (End)

CONTENTS

ACKNOWLEDGMENTS

To all those gentle souls who have graciously given tokens of love, hope, and kind considerations to others.

0 Preface

Last time, Jack dashes away from the abandoned Widow's Cloister as he sees the AnCors approaching. Does he escape? Or do the AnCors catch him?

Jack wonders if it really was Queenie he had seen at the Men's Prison. If it was Queenie, should he look for her? Would she remember him? Is it worth it or should he accept his current situation, get away, and not take risks?

Skipper Courtly reveals to his son, Pip, his intentions about harnessing the power of the ghost in the dungeon of his new castle. Has Skipper become so bored with his world that he is now reaching for supernatural powers?

Skipper is creating a throne room, where Mr. Bjorn Esterday is forced to sit on the floor before interviewing his highness Skipper Courtly. Skipper seems focused on ensuring everybody knows that he is elevated (figuratively and literally) while others are beneath him.

Elder James urgently guides the sisters and Eldress away from their convent. From a safe distance they attempt to carefully observe the unprotected cloister, only to find that it is suddenly being overrun and occupied by the AnCors.

Elder James suggests a wide detour before heading back to the Earth Farmer Monastery. Where does he take them?

1 CHAPTER Year 2036: Castle Dungeon (Continuous Ch 43)

Skipper already had candles carefully arranged to light the foyer, in anticipation of Bjorn's arrival. Bjorn followed Skipper, but pressed his hand against the wall to brace himself as he stepped down the damp mossy stairs. Skipper turned to Bjorn, stopping in front of the heavy door leading to the heart of the basement.

"Yesterday, as you know, I scrutinized the workmen and selected a few to trust with my 'Museo d'arte'. I instructed them to neatly arrange all the objects up against one wall down here, remember?"

1

"Yes," Bjorn replied, "I remember like it was yesterday."

Skipper continued, "But, now you can see..." Skipper opened the door with a couple of hearty tugs. As the door creaked open, Skipper slipped inside, beckoning Bjorn to follow him.

Inside, the dark basement, Skipper fumbled on the wall, searching for a switch.

He found it.

Dim flickering lights barely illuminated the center of the room. Bjorn's eyes were adjusting from the bright day outside to this poorly lit interior and now he saw what was before him.

Skipper looked at Bjorn for a reaction, "You see it?"

Bjorn nodded. All the objects, which he remembered being neatly arranged along one wall, were now wildly tossed about into a scrambled heap. Standing in the midst of the haphazard jumble of carved wooden statuary, a large coffin stood

2

upright on one end.

"Sure is a mess," Bjorn stated simply.

He walked to one piece laying on its side and tried to pick it up, at first with one hand, then two.

"Is this wood? It's as heavy as a boulder. Too much for an average guy like me to lift. Who did this?" Bjorn asked.

"Who? Who? Who? Mr. Esterday, don't you see? It is the evidence of the castle spirit. The ghost has come out in the night and tossed everything all over the place. And there is his trademark in the center. Standing right there. Oh, it's breathtaking," Skipper announced triumphantly.

Skipper turned away to shout up the stairs. In response, came the clomping of burly workmen wending their way down the slippery steps. He had permitted a specific few to clean the place up yesterday, and now he was permitting them to enter his dungeon again, today.

Skipper barked, "Straighten it all up! I want everything neatly lined up against that wall, like you did yesterday!"

One workman replied, "Mr. Courtly, sir. It took us all day to get it done. If you want us to do it again, we'll need several hours."

"Yes, yes, yes. I know it takes time. I need the stage to be set perfectly so that this reporter can document it." Skipper summarily clapped his hands twice to punctuate his order, "Get on with it!"

And the workmen started to figure out how to untangle the mess which lay before them.

"Sir?" Bjorn asked, "Does your ghost have a name?"

"Mr. Esterday, the spirits are beyond syntax. Supernatural beings don't have names humans can pronounce."

"Huh," Bjorn muttered to himself, "Well, 'ghost' could be a name..."

Skipper turned to Bjorn, "You are being given this extraordinary privilege. You shall chronicle my night in this dungeon. The legend promises that whoever overcomes the force of the ghost will inherit great powers. You will return tomorrow after the men have straightened everything out, to document my transformation which will occur after my encounter with the spirit."

2 CHAPTER Year 2036: Sarah's Condo (Continuous Ch 44)

At Sarah's humble apartment, Bjorn was busily making Sarah a pot of tea for the two of them to share. Sarah sat on the sofa by the coffee table, with her elbows on her knees holding her forehead.

"It's all right, Bjorn," Sarah tried to be analytical about it all. "I look forward to teaching in the Fall. I mean I... it's all right. It was just a temporary assignment. I didn't need to pay off all my debts this summer. No big deal." Sarah leaned back into the sofa. "I just wish I knew where Alexandra found that information. I can't believe it was just hanging around in the paper files."

Bjorn placed a tray down on the coffee table with cream, sugar, a tea pot and two cups.

"You mean the file that got you fired? Lucky losing your job was all that happened to you yesterday."

He sat down on the small couch next to Sarah and poured a cup of tea, handing it to her. "You know, corporations routinely eliminate annoying employees...and some just disappear..."

Sarah accepted the tea, pouring a spot of cream and adding a dash of sugar into her cup. "Please, don't... That's just a rumor."

Bjorn gave himself a cup, taking it black, "Fine. It does happen, though."

"I don't know why it bugs me, but Alexandra seems like a simple quiet, naïve girl. How would she know the value of the information in that file? Anyway," Sarah changed subjects, "the legal office said after I finish up some work at the castle, I must pick up my final paycheck. The place had a cabled computer network back in the 1980's and need it fixed."

"Good luck with bringing that thing back to life!" Bjorn quipped.

"Anyway, they will let me know before the end of this week when I'll get security clearance to re-enter castle grounds. So…maybe we could do dinner here after your interview?"

Bjorn took a sip, put down his cup, and then put his hand on Sarah's knee. "Sarah, I'm going to tell King Skipper that I cannot go to his castle tomorrow to document his ridiculous transformation. I'd rather spend the day with you. We could have lunch and dinner that way…"

"Bjorn, you have to go tomorrow. You're on his schedule. In his calendar. Besides, they don't realize you and I know each other. They fired me for some stupid reason. They could fire you if you don't do what Skipper wants. Don't risk your job. It will seem weird to them if you just stop covering the series on the castle. Don't you think?"

3 CHAPTER Year 2036: A Broken Nail (Continuous Ch 45)

Determined to fulfill her obligations, especially when her final paycheck is dependent upon her completing this job, Sarah Paradise arrived at the Castle site along with the construction workers. She clutched the device, which gave her security clearance for today only.

Slung around her shoulder was a bag containing computer tools for installing old fashioned late 20th century computer cables. She had located a supplier who sold Skipper Courtly the last of his stock.

She scampered up the steps of the main entrance and peered into the high ceilinged cavernous foyer. She found the foreman looking at his blue prints and directing his queued-up workers to receive their assignments for that day. She stood in line with the other workers. After waiting her turn, she approached the foreman, smiling.

"Hello. I'm Sarah Paradise. I am here to set up an antique computer network. Could you point me to where I'm supposed to go?"

The foreman checked his list and saw Sarah's name, then looked over the blueprints to see where she was assigned to work.

"Yup. I gatta warn you that Mr. Courtly is just a little sensitive about certain areas, here. I wouldn't go exploring or anything. He'd bite your head off," the foreman stated.

"Well, this is what I got from the main office this morning."

Sarah showed the foreman the hand

held device with its redmail notice giving Sarah security access authority to all areas of the castle for that day only.

The foreman looked at her.

"We got a delivery of spooled cables yesterday. Is that for your job? What would you use those for?"

Sarah explained, "The way they used to install computer networks back in the late 20th century, was to run cables to a main server that was out of sight. The cables would go through the walls or ceilings or floors and then power up the monitors where the people would sit and use them."

"Wow," the foreman replied, "no wonder he wanted those in before we finish sealing up the walls. So, you had to physically connect those suckers? That is old fashioned!"

Sarah shrugged.

"And he can pay for it," the foreman offered. "Not like today where we can communicate and recharge just by exposing our devices to sunlight."

He pointed out to Sarah the basement on the blueprints, then indicated the staircase leading down to the heavy door.

"My men just finished cleaning the place up last night. Your delivery is at the top of those stairs over there. So, it's all ready for whatever you need to do. I gatta oversee my guys on the other side of the property, so I'll leave you to it. The front door will stay opened all day, so you can leave when you're done."

He paused as he shut down his blueprints to take with him, then turned back to her. "I'd get in and out before Mr. Courtly gets here, Miss Paradise. I know you have clearance, but Mr. Courtly may yell at you just the same. Consider it friendly advice, is all."

"Oh don't worry," she said as she headed toward the stairs, in the direction the foreman indicated. "After I install this cable, I'll be out of here."

Gingerly stepping over the large coil of computer cables at the top of the stairs, and carefully squishing down the mossy steps, Sarah found the basement door had been propped open and the dim bulbs were already on. She had to take a moment to let her eyes adjust to the weak lighting as she slipped her bag of tools off her shoulder and onto the ground.

From everything Bjorn had told her, she was expecting a mess, but as the foreman said, his men had cleaned and straightened out all the statues. They were neatly lined up in rows. Good. It would be easier for her to work in a clean environment.

Luckily, a rickety ladder was already there. She glanced up, surprised to see no cobwebs, which she hoped meant no creepy spiders would interrupt her work. She squinted her eyes to scrutinize the old cables which seemed badly frayed, hanging from the ceiling, and thought she should investigate them first.

Sarah cautiously climbed up the ladder and onto the sturdy, shadowy, stone ledge to examine the connections up near the ceiling.

Her hands scraped against the rough rock and she wished she had brought gloves with her. On her hands and knees, she crept along the two foot wide ledge, looking up. One hand on the ledge, one hand groping for the cables above her as she felt for the frayed wires needing repair.

No wonder those antique computers were not working upstairs.

As her hand traced the cables, feeling them, Sarah tried to figure out what she could splice and patch and what she would totally need to replace. Of course a patch job would get her out faster.

Yes, she decided patching was the way to go. She measured what lengths she would need to cut from the coil of cable back at the top of the stairs.

Then, she broke a nail.

The jagged edge of her fingernail bothered her. She kneeled a moment on her knees, bracing one hand on the ledge in front of her, and the other hand, holding the cable like one used to do when standing during rush-hour in an old subway car.

She was about to search her pockets for a nail file when she was hit by something on the back of her head. Without having time to react, Sarah slumped awkwardly onto the ledge, her body lay motionless in the deep silent shadows.

4 CHAPTER Year 2036: Tantrum On The Scaffold (Continuous Ch 46)

Bjorn was on Skipper Courtly's calendar. He recalled Sarah's advice to keep his word and his appointment to cover the vapid story of an over-indulged self-centered rich man.

He walked along the castle path.

Ah, that lake. So placid. Almost makes visiting this place worth it. He noticed a young couple had taken a tiny row boat out onto the middle of the lake. Romantic, he thought. A short distance away, that same fishing boat was still beached on the shore. Gentle waves

17

lifted the worn hull from time to time.

As Bjorn approached the front of the grand castle, he noticed that although it was afternoon, and the construction equipment was there, he didn't hear the sounds of busy workers. There was no drilling, no hammering, and no shouting.

He took the steps two at a time, and found that the massive front doors were open wide. The force field was off.

Where was everybody?

He wandered inside. "Hello?" he called.

He stood a moment in the echoing foyer and waited. When nobody came, he ventured inside the castle, heading toward King Skipper's favorite place, the throne room.

From just outside the throne chamber, Bjorn noticed scaffolding had been set up, nearly blocking the entrance.

Bjorn looked up to see a half-done, high, vaulted ceiling decorated with the romantic paintings of pink lined cumulous clouds, golden shafts of sun rays dancing between brightly plumed flying birds and butterflies. And of course, a serene soft blue sky.

Its grandeur made the viewer feel small and insignificant. Bjorn recognized at once that this was a medieval Venetian ploy, a copy of that old psychological trick of intimidation the Doges of Venice used to play on their visitors.

Back in Italy, the Doges would never see their visitors right away. A visitor would be asked to wait in one room, then ushered into consecutively smaller and more plain cell-like rooms. The last chamber would be manned by a panel of somber ebony-clad silent men who simply stared at the visitor.

After many hours during which he was offered neither food nor drink, this confused thoroughly intimidated visitor, would be ceremoniously marched into the shockingly huge lush throne room. The lavish splendor of the Doge's elevated throne would undoubtedly render this visitor speechless, unable to make any petition.

This process was done to underscore that the man on the throne was closer to the heavens than the visitor and thereby had greater power. The Doge did this to limit the visitor requests by shocking them with the sudden heaven-like display of wealth and power.

Bjorn smiled wondering what the Earth Farmers would think of all this godless pomp. It was total rubbish, of course, to a sturdy man-of-faith like Bjorn, who knew any person could pray to God. On the other hand, Bjorn admitted to himself, that the political theatrics which propped up the authority of the Doge had lasted a millennium.

Skipper Courtly's version of this display was captivating.

Bjorn doubted anybody visiting King Skippie would mistake him for a man possessing any powers of an intimidating demi-deity no matter how many ethereal clouds were painted on the vaulted dome ceiling.

Bjorn smiled as he figured how to work that detail into his Lifestyles feature, somehow.

He made his way under the scaffolding, through the plastic curtain and into the throne room, stepping on a large crinkled drop-cloth. Now, he thought he heard the voices of people calling out.

Before him, he caught sight of the foreman and the other workmen surrounding the scaffolding at the far end of the grand chamber.

They were all looking up, but the ceiling on that side of the room, had not yet been finished, so what were they looking at?

Recognizing Bjorn, the foreman, rushed over to him with a smile, obviously happy to see him.

Then, Bjorn saw it.

At the very top of the scaffolding was Skipper Courtly, clutching his violin, having a tantrum.

"Sir, you are in danger of falling. Please be careful," the foreman called up to him, then turned to Bjorn to whisper, "That old man won't move. I've been looking for Mr. Courtly for an hour. Can't find him anywhere. Then wham! A minute ago, he shows up on the top of the scaffolding, violating every construction safety regulation there is!"

"I will not come down! You are all fiends!" Skipper shouted, making the men at the base squint and hastily step back as his words were accompanied with a spray of spittle.

Bjorn called up to Skipper Courtly, "Mr. Courtly? I'm here to follow up on your ghost-guy. Like you asked. Remember?"

Bjorn followed the Foreman toward the precarious scaffolding, now shaking with the fury that Skipper displayed as he waved his arms.

"You wangled your way into the dungeon. Sure. But you are not getting your grubby hands on my magical violin!" Skipper clutched the instrument to his chest protectively.

One of the other workers called up, "Sir, we just want to see you safe. To help you down."

Skipper shouted, "Silence!"

One of the other workers murmured, "Well, if that guy falls off and breaks his neck, I guess we don't get paid, so might as well just go home, now."

Bjorn called again, "Mr. Courtly, don't you have an appointment to keep with your spirit so he can transform you with amazing powers?" Bjorn was almost sarcastic, but that got Skipper to stop snarling at the workers beneath him and look right at Bjorn.

"Yes. Yes. Yes," Skipper said as if suddenly he were a different person.

He started to scramble down but had difficulty holding onto the scaffolding as he clung to the violin. He kicked away any worker who tried to help him. The foreman, and the men Skipper had earlier allowed into the basement, stepped forward and formed a human staircase that Skipper used to clumsily ease himself to safety.

Without saying thank you to the men who assisted him, Skipper pranced to Bjorn, who was rapidly making notes.

The foreman whispered to Bjorn when he found a free moment, "Thanks, we couldn't get back to work with him up there!" and he proceeded to organize his crew.

Skipper seeing the Foreman talking to Bjorn became irate and snarled to the Foreman, "There! You have your absurd scaffold back. Now... Get to work!"

Bjorn shrugged at the foreman, trying to convey he was simpatico with what the crew was going through. The foreman got on his communication device and ordered men across the property to get busy.

In the distance, Bjorn heard machinery begin to power up.

Excitedly, Skipper turned to Bjorn and said, "You should have come earlier. I had them clean up the basement again. You need to look at it. Mr. Esterday, my plan to lure the ghost to me is working.

Actually working!"

As Skipper and Bjorn crossed through the grand foyer, it became increasingly difficult to understand each other over the loud construction noises, making Skipper very frustrated when he could not be heard.

He set down his violin in a chair at the top of the stairs leading to the basement, and took both his hands to form a cone to shout at Bjorn, "Follow me downstairs where I can hear you."

Bjorn indicated that he understood and followed Skipper.

Bjorn and Skipper carefully stepped over a pile of coiled computer cable to descend the mossy steps.

A couple of construction workers crossed the floor on their way to resume working in the throne room. They accidentally bumped the chair holding Skipper's violin. One worker saw it, gasped, and reached to catch the instrument before it hit the hard floor. Luckily, he did catch it, but by one string.

The string snapped.

"Better the string than the whole body breaking," offered his companion.

The other nodded and replaced the violin on the chair, but this time with the strings facing the cushion so the broken one wouldn't show. They both furtively looked around to make sure there were no witnesses and then quickly hurried on their way.

Meanwhile, down in the stairwell on the way to the basement, Bjorn started asking his interview questions.

"How much is this construction costing you per day, do you estimate?"

They stopped in front of the now closed basement door.

Skipper was about to answer when right behind them, Mr. Atsushi appeared, following them, interrupting.

"Oh, glad I found you," Atsushi said to Skipper.

"Off to play squash, again, my man?"

Skipper quipped trying to give the impression of a firm but jovial leader for Bjorn to record in his Lifestyles story.

"I just stopped by the castle to get you to sign some papers," Mr. Atsushi smiled, then made eye contact with Bjorn with a polite nod.

"Yes, yes, yes. I'll sign them. You're always asking me to sign something. I told you at the office I'd sign them and I will when I have time. Where are you off to, Atsushi?"

"I'll tell you what, Skipper, I will leave the papers on the side table by the top of the stairs. I'll even leave a pen so you can scribble your autograph. Later, after my match with Pip, I'll swing back by and scan-file them for you." He turned around and headed cautiously back up the slippery stairs. Skipper started to tug at the basement door to open it.

At the top of the stairs, the lawyer turned around to say one final thing, "Oh, by the way, that foreman was looking for you."

With a grunt, Skipper slowly pulled open the heavy dungeon door.

"Who was that?" Bjorn asked Skipper.

Skipper was taken aback that Bjorn didn't know every single acquaintance of Skipper's. Skipper explained, "That's my attorney."

"Has he been with Courtly Dynamics Corporation for very long?" Bjorn asked.

"Mostly," Skipper replied curtly, "he babysits my son, Pip. He even signed up for an art class with Pip to help my son pass the class."

"That's a bit above and beyond your average staff attorney," Bjorn persisted. "Sounds like your Mr. Atsushi is part of the Courtly family."

Skipper stepped over the threshold into the basement. He hoped to finally put an end to this line of questioning and get back to discussing how he will acquire supernatural powers.

"Oh, I suppose," Skipper blandly stated, "he's very useful. He's also the one who tipped me off to the spirit of this castle and agrees with me that I can harness that power." He took a breath, satisfied that he had turned the tide of the conversation. "Oh, that's right, the spirit. Now, where shall I begin about my plan to become one with the spirit?"

Bjorn asked, "May I ask, sir, how did you discover that your brother died in that train accident when a body was never found?"

Annoyed, Skipper replied, "All that speculation is nonsense just because no bodies were found. Those victims were discovered out in the open, so obviously wildlife had dragged away the carnage. I can't be blamed for that. I mean, why won't those people just take my word for it? Jack is dead!" Skipper paused, and then his eyes widened.

"Oh. Oh. Oh," he whispered, "do you think the ghost is trying to contact me with a message from my dead brother?"

Skipper's communication device started to glow.

"Wait,wait! I must climb back up the stairs! You see, it's a weak signal on my com-device. Good thing we didn't close that door yet."

Bjorn nodded as Skipper squeezed past him and went up a few steps. Of course, Bjorn turned his back, but stayed near the mouth of the opening to try and listen in as best he could.

Skipper angrily barked into his communication device, "Pip! I am your father! Do not accuse me of throwing your inheritance away. The rewards of this renovation will payback 100 fold!"

Skipper continued with frothy spittle dotting his chin as he inhaled to increase his volume, "Priceless, I tell you! If you had any sense, you'd see. I will harness the power and I am doing this for all of us. No. Don't try to talk me out of it, Pip. I must enter the dungeon! Now! And you know I won't get your signal in there, so I will speak to you again once I emerge imbued with power tomorrow....No...I won't answer. I won't be able to. Bye." And with a sweeping arm gesture, he disconnected the call.

Skipper walked back down the stairs to Bjorn, "Would you like to go inside the dungeon, Mr. Esterday, or continue the interview here at the door?"

5 CHAPTER- Year 2036: Lock Him In (Continuous Ch 47)

For some reason, standing on these mossy stone steps felt odd. Bjorn was not one who normally had "gut feelings", but something felt wrong, almost spooky, and he couldn't logically figure out why.

Without entering, Bjorn leaned forward to look past Skipper, into the shadowy basement. He got chills, and he became more aware of a dank odor. He did not have any jaunty quips ready to fire away. This time, when Skipper stood at the mouth of this cave-like room, it really did feel as if they were about to enter an ancient dungeon.

Somehow, Bjorn would have to shake off this feeling if he was to give his editor, Sammy, the information needed to run a fluffy Lifestyles story. Sometimes, he felt more comfortable falling back into his find-the-facts reporter mode.

They were still standing at the entrance of the basement, but maybe if Bjorn just got to it, he could get the information he needed, then get out of that creepy place.

"So," Bjorn started right in, "I've heard that all the Courtly Corporations have made agreements with some of the farming communities."

"Agreements?" Skipper asked.

"Yes. Agreements. For example, dealing with waste disposal. Can you share what the terms are between Courtly and Earth Farmers on waste, Mr. Courtly?

"That one was set up by Jack," Skipper responded casually, "My brother had a soft heart, you see. A soft head to go with it. No head for business. All those agreements were bad business and I've had to deal with those things for the last few years." He took an impatient breath, "Enough office gossip. You are not here for that, Mr. Esterday. Let us harness the power of the spirit world."

"The acoustics of this place seem...," Bjorn commented.

"Yes, yes, yes. It's almost as if the room is breathing, Mr. Esterday. Yes. The magic is very strong right now."

"The workers cleaned it up yesterday?"

"The men straightened everything up last night and it's been untouched until this moment. This dungeon is alive, ripe with heightened spiritual activity."

Bjorn muttered more to himself, "There must be some logical explanation for these statues to become scattered over..."

"Oh there is!" Skipper clapped his hands with delight, "It's the ghost of the castle. I shall remain here for the duration of the night. Please see yourself out."

"Myself out? I thought you wanted me to chronicle your transformation."

"No, no, no," Skipper scolded annoyed as his voice rose with increasingly dramatic inflections, "Your job is to describe what you see, what you feel, and how I appear to you. Then you will return tomorrow, let me out and be prepared for a mighty force to greet you, Mr. Esterday."

He then toned his voice down, continuing in a matter-of-fact manner, "I am not risking having YOU steal the powers away by sharing this experience with me. Throw the bolt as you leave, so you are witness to locking me in the dungeon all night long."

"Lock you in?" Bjorn shook his head, "No way. I'm here to observe and interview, not participate. I just don't feel right about locking anybody in anywhere, Mr. Courtly."

They both looked up to see the foreman

coming down the stairs, waving a contract device in his hand.

"I don't mean to interrupt, Sir, but we'll need your signature, again, please." He handed a stylus to Skipper along with his clipboard-sized contract unit, which had an electronic waiver floating on it.

"Sign, sign, sign," Skipper grabbed the unit and writing implement, "Sometimes it's on paper, sometimes it's on this device, but it's always something to sign." He scribbled his signature and shoved it back at the foreman with a snort of disdain.

The foreman remained, "You know, I actually came down here earlier, looking for…"

Skipper interrupted over his sentence, "Mr. Esterday, return tomorrow to unlock the door and record my new powers for all your readers and viewers at The Daily Memo."

"As I said, Mr. Courtly, I'm not comfortable…"

"Enough. I have spoken," Skipper barked adopting a very regal expression.

"I'd lock you in if it meant we could get our work done, you crazy..." The foreman muttered to himself so only Bjorn could hear. He made eye contact with Bjorn, then stopped talking.

Skipper turned to him, "Mr. Foreman. Pay attention as I will now hereby give you new orders. Tonight, you will lock me in so I may conquer this ghost, wrestle him for his powers and become transformed. Mr. Esterday, see yourself out, I have no patience for a doubter."

"Sir," Bjorn protested to Skipper, "I..." and then he stopped talking, shrugged his shoulders and turned toward the foreman speaking quietly, "I really don't think it's a good idea to lock him in here."

The foreman whispered to Bjorn, "I'll lock the outer bolt for now, just so he can hear it slide shut from the outside...and to get him to shut up. Then I'll unlock it before I leave with the crew tonight."

Skipper barked, "Stop huddling, you two! You both have your orders!" He glared at the foreman, "You there, lock me in!" Then he turned to Bjorn, "And you, return tomorrow to document my transformation, you doubter. Out. Show yourselves out and tomorrow you will become believers in my new authority."

"Yes, sir," the foreman spoke clearly.

Quickly, both Bjorn and the foreman exited the basement, pushing the heavy door shut behind them, leaving Skipper Courtly inside.

The foreman threw the old medieval style metal bolt with a loud dull clang. He shook his head, relieved that Skipper's mad-man antics would be contained for a while. Finally, his workers could finish their shift uninterrupted by any more stunts or capricious demands. He nodded a good-bye to Bjorn, then bounded up the stairs.

In the distance, as Bjorn headed to the front door to let himself out, he heard the foreman shout to his men.

"All right, crew. We lost a lot of time earlier because of that stunt our customer pulled up on our scaffold. Good news is we won't have any more interruptions from him for a while. C'mon! We still need to deliver on time or we don't get paid!"

The men scurried to their posts.

Bjorn let himself out and descended the wide marble steps at the front door. He felt relieved to feel his feet on solid ground, again.

"What a place. How did a man like that get entrusted with the Courtly empire?"

He struggled as he tried to figure out how he could make this article flattering, which is what both Sammy, his editor, and Skipper Courtly were expecting.

Bjorn wistfully took a long look across the lake at that little tethered fishing boat, representing a deadline-free afternoon, beneath the dusky sky. Pink and golden rays of the setting sun twinkled across the water.

Bjorn mused that a moonlit boat ride might be a very romantic idea. He decided to propose it to Sarah as soon as he saw her. It would take both their minds off their recent stresses.

Then, Bjorn got into his vehicle and left. He really should spend some time with Sarah. He decided to surprise her by making dinner tonight.

Did he have enough to write his article now, or would he really have to return to indulge Skipper Courtly?

6 CHAPTER Year 2036: The Florist's Shop (Continuous Ch 48)

"Sarah should get a reward for putting up with that family," Bjorn reasoned as he finished picking up groceries.

He walked along the sidewalk to his vehicle. Before getting in, he glanced up and smiled at the full platinum moon gleaming in a cloudless night sky.

He realized he had paused in front of a florist shop. It was a tiny boutique with cheerful displays in the window. And it was still open.

Bjorn figured a bouquet, along with

ingredients to make a fantastic dinner, would be just the surprise that would show Sarah he appreciates her. Just because.

He walked into the small shop, with his bag of groceries in one hand and his communication device in his ear. He contacted Sarah.

"It's me, again. This is the fourth message I've left you, so I am picking up dinner and I'll be heading over your place soon. You are going to like what I'm making tonight."

He disconnected the line and then noticed that the florist was busy on her own phone. So Bjorn quietly looked around at the various floral arrangements while she took her call.

After a few moments, he found a display he liked, made eye contact with the florist, smiled, and pointed to the one he wanted to buy.

Obviously, the florist was engulfed in a conversation she didn't want to be having, but had to, so kept talking while she assembled the flowers for Bjorn's order.

"Yes. It's like a cylinder," she spoke into her communication device. "I know it's your first big account, and that's why I'm here, to help." She looked at Bjorn and asked, "Do you want baby's breath with this?"

Bjorn nodded.

Back into the phone, the woman said, "No. I was speaking with a customer here in the shop, who is being very understanding that I'm talking to you on a big account with a demanding bride." She winked at Bjorn as she was finishing up his order.

Bjorn smiled to himself. Everybody has to work and every job has its challenges.

"Okay," the woman continued into the com device, "If you want to know how many cubic feet of water that circular pond will hold, you need volume, which is Pi times "r" squared. Yes.... Yes... radius squared times "h" or height... Hold on for a second."

Then, she looked at Bjorn, presenting him with a beautifully wrapped bouquet of blue crocus, sunny yellow double-bloom peonies, and pink tulips abundantly filled out with masses of baby's breath.

She paused a moment before handing it to him, then reached under the counter to pick out a tiny plush baby bear and tied a big bow around its waist, attaching it to the bouquet.

"Sir?" She smiled at Bjorn, "The toy is on the house. I appreciate your patience. Will there be anything else?"

7 CHAPTER Year 2036: A Note On The Door (Continuous Ch 49)

Bjorn assumed Sarah was taking one of her long baths. That must be why she was not answering her com device. She needed to forget about the stresses of recent events.

He arrived at Sarah's condo door, arms filled with groceries and a bouquet of flowers sticking out of the top of the bag. About to knock, he paused, noticing a note posted to the front of Sarah's door, addressed to him.

He shifted his bag to one arm, plucked off the note with the other hand and read it.

"B- I left you a com-message, but you didn't pick up. So, I'm leaving you this note just in case you came by before our dinner date. They just gave me clearance to work at the castle for today only. The sooner I finish that gig, the sooner I get paid. I'll take the bus and walk there. I figured, since you are interviewing him today, come find me when you are done. We can leave together. Okay? Love, S."

Confused, Bjorn looked at his communication device display and saw he had missed a message from Sarah sent earlier that morning.

Suddenly, it dawned on him.

Clutching the heavy bag of groceries, Bjorn dashed to his car, threw the groceries into the back and tossed the flowers in the passenger seat. He peeled out of his parking space and his vehicle roared forward onto the deserted road.

With one hand directing his path, he

tried to contact Skipper's communication device with the other.

He got a com-message and just disconnected.

Then he remembered the call Skipper had with his son, Pip, and that com reception was dicey at the castle.

Was Sarah in that basement? Is that why she wasn't answering her com? Was Skipper aware of what was about to happen?

He raced non-stop to get there before it was too late. Wheels screeching, he swerved around every corner. The grocery bag flipped over, spilling everything out across the back seat. Beside him, the bouquet was tossed wildly. The dangling stuffed animal, roped to the bouquet with a ribbon, rolled around like a staked tetherball with every bump and turn. He shouted a voice command and the safety harness snapped the bouquet in place.

8 CHAPTER Year 2036: Before It Is Too Late (Continuous Ch 50)

The full moon was at its brightest, lighting his path as he raced up the dark road. He tried one last time to contact Sarah, but to no avail. Now, he was unable to even leave a message because her recording device was full, most likely from messages he himself had left.

His vehicle bumped up the unfinished castle footpath with the lake water glistening like diamonds in the wake of one large reflecting moon beam. He searched to see if the shaft of moonlight hit that little tethered boat he always looked for.

Yes.

There it was bobbing away, still tethered so it wouldn't float off, rocked by the lapping waves beneath it, but the beach along the shore had disappeared.

Adrenaline high, he was thankful the force field had not been activated, yet. That must mean the crew was still there.

Bjorn scrambled up to the huge open entrance and burst in. Lights in the foyer were on and bright. He shouted for the foreman.

Curious, the foreman poked his head out from behind a corner, packing his things for the night.

"Most of the crew have already left, Mr. Esterday. What brings you back here? I was just about to lock up," the foreman said as he casually ambled toward Bjorn.

"Did a woman come by? To do some kind of a project here today?" Bjorn asked, panic lacing his voice.

The foreman instinctively shook his head no, but then seemed to remember something, "Oh, yeah. She did. I even came down to the basement to see if she was still there, but I saw you and Mr. Courtly, so forgot about it."

"When?"

"Oh, um. Early. First thing. I mean she was doing something with old fashioned cables that are before my time. My men only install the stuff we use today."

"Where is she?"

"She must have left because she wasn't in the basement. What's the problem?" The foreman was wondering why Bjorn was so anxious.

"But," Bjorn pointed to the dark stairs leading to the basement. "That pile of cables looks untouched. She'd never leave a job undone. She came here by bus. She was expecting to leave with me. Are you sure you saw her leave?"

Offended, the foreman stated, "Look, she's not part of my crew. I didn't see her leave, but I'm not responsible for…"

Slowly, Bjorn asked, "Did you unlock the basement door so Skipper Courtly could get out?"

"Oh!" the foreman remembered, "Thanks for reminding me. No, I'll unlock the door, now."

Seeing Bjorn race past him down the stairs, the foreman commented, "What's the rush?"

Bjorn shouted over his shoulder, "C'mon help me! Before it's too late!" and he disappeared down the stone steps.

The foreman followed.

9 CHAPTER Year 2036: A Broken String (Continuous Ch 51)

Bjorn put his ear to the heavy dungeon door and listened. He didn't like what he heard and tugged at the bolt.

The foreman, not far behind, scooped up a hard hat with a light on it. The foreman popped the helmet onto his head as the light flipped on. He raced to join Bjorn at the bottom of the stairs.

Water was seeping through the edges of the door.

"It's sweating?" the foreman commented, a look of horror crossed his face. He was clearly not expecting to see this. "And Mr. Courtly refused to allow my crew to do a full foundation inspection. We would have known about this –and been able to fix it- if we were allowed to survey..."

"Is that light waterproof?" Bjorn asked, indicating the foreman's hardhat light.

"Yeah," the Forman responded distractedly as he started to examine the leaking water illuminated by the beam on his hardhat, "Only current safety equipment on this job."

Bjorn shouted into the door, "Hey! Mr. Courtly!", then Bjorn pressed his ear against the heavy door. Dull thuds were heard in reply.

While the foreman aimed his hardhat lamp onto the door handle, he tugged to find the door was too heavy to budge. Bjorn moved in, gripped the handle, and put his back into it as both men dragged the door open.

Out poured a wall of freezing black water, crashing over them, abruptly releasing the pressure from inside the basement, filling up the stairwell.

Murky water slammed around them, dragging them under as they fought to regain balance. Statues rolled and banged against the stone dungeon walls with every relentless wave. The two men stumbled into each other, hands searching for a brace against the wall, feet slipping on the mossy steps beneath them as they fought the oncoming force of tumbling whirlpools. Waves rolled up the steps as if reaching for more victims, dragging along the barely alive Mr. Courtly.

Halfway up the stairs, the men braced their backs against the wall and lifted Skipper Courtly up so that his face was out of the water. Skipper gasped for breath, sputtering. His eyes were squeezed shut, arms flailing.

Bjorn shouted, "Can you haul him up by yourself?"

"Sure," the foreman replied grabbing Skipper Courtly under his arms, and dragging him backward up the stairs, fighting the weight of the water.

"Great," Bjorn stated as he grabbed the foreman's light-hardhat, "I'll take that," Bjorn said commandeering the flashlight helmet.

As he dragged the limp half-conscious, sputtering rich man up the stairs, the foreman shouted back at Bjorn, "Why do you need it? You're not going back down there? Are you?"

Before ducking in, Bjorn shouted back, "She might be inside. I have to know."

The foreman struggled to haul Skipper up each step until he could lay Mr. Courtly out on the floor at the top of the landing.

Once safely sprawled out, Skip Courtly muttered, "I could have drowned, I could have drowned, I could have drowned..."

The foreman, ran to the pile of supplies where he got his lighted hard hat earlier, and grabbed another one, placing it firmly on his head. He started to descend the steps to see if Bjorn needed further assistance.

Opening the door had released the pressure of water being contained within the stone basement walls. The water had leveled out somewhat and was lapping now around the foreman's knees.

Bjorn had already waded far inside the dark basement. He could barely walk as large objects floated around him, occasionally bumping into him. The water, now at chest level, had made him buoyant so that his feet barely touched the dungeon floor as he made his way through.

He adjusted his hardhat light and anxiously looked around at all the floating objects.

Then he heard a moan.

The beam of light from the hardhat, whipped around, down, no up. Scanning the ceiling, Bjorn recalled there was a ledge up there. Could it be she was up there? His light caught the ledge. He saw a hand move, and a bit of Sarah's hair in a crevice near the top of the wall.

"There she is!"

Shoving the floating statues aside, Bjorn spotted the top of the coffin just above water, standing upright below the high ledge.

"At least you'll be useful, now," he said to himself as he climbed out of the water onto the top of the upright coffin. He carefully eased himself to a standing position. Slowly, he reached up. He could touch the ledge.

"Sarah! Sarah! Can you hear me, Sarah!'

He heard a faint rustling. She coughed.

"You are surrounded by water. Move slowly, Sarah. I'm reaching for your hand."

Bjorn searched for her hand along the ledge.

Nothing. He tried to stretch a bit further, but could only feel rough stone.

Then, Sarah's hand landed on top of his.

"Bjorn?" she gasped.

"Yes! Sarah!" His voice revealed his relief for having found Sarah alive.

"Are you hurt?"

"My head," she said, "Bright light."

"That's my hardhat. Come to the light. Slowly."

The swirling objects continued to bang and bump ominously around the room as they collided with each other and the walls.

"Listen, Sarah, and hold onto me. We are going to drop into water," Bjorn instructed.

Sarah tried to sit up, accidentally knocking her communication device off her ear. She heard it plunk into the swirling chaos below her. Useless.

Slowly, Sarah, guided by Bjorn, held on to his hand as they splashed down into the icy cold water together. In the light cast by Bjorn's hardhat, she saw weather beaten faces of statues move toward her and then float away. Getting a mouthful of water, caused Sarah to cough. Bjorn pulled her close, holding her tightly around her waist. He felt her shivering uncontrollably.

When he was able to make his way to the flooded stairs, the foreman switched on his light and shouted, "I'm here if you need me, Bjorn."

Bjorn saw the foreman's light and used it as a marker as he floated toward the open dungeon door.

"We are coming toward you," Bjorn shouted.

The foreman, who was pushing away statues now floating up into the stairwell, kept a path clear for both Bjorn and the woman with him.

Once Bjorn made it to the entrance, Sarah in tow, he braced her as they both slowly waded up the narrow steps. Behind them, the foreman worked to try and close the door, but couldn't move it with the force of the water ebbing and flowing against it. Giving up on the door, the foreman turned to help Bjorn bring Sarah up to the landing.

Bjorn didn't realize how much energy would be drained from him doing this.

Almost at the top, they were greeted by the angry voice of Skipper Courtly screaming, "Who did this to my violin! Who broke a string!"

Crawling out onto the landing, all three of them collapsed, ignoring Skipper Courtly's shrieks of outrage. Sarah, gasped for air, exhausted and wounded. Bjorn, adrenaline crashing, handed the hardhat back to the foreman with a breathless, "Thanks".

The foreman, slumped to the ground.

It had already been a hard day and his men had to work late because of Mr. Courtly's antics... and now this. As he sat there exhausted, the foreman was greeted by a dripping Skipper Courtly, crawling over, waving his violin like a flag.

"Did you do this damage?" he demanded shoving the broken string in front of the foreman's face.

10 CHAPTER Year 2036: Hospital Room (Continuous Ch 52)

In the darkness of her hospital room, Sarah Paradise tried to get comfortable. She wished she could be in her own bed, clutching her own pillow, wearing her own night clothes.

Instead, her head rested uncomfortably on a hypoallergenic block of foam. All she could hear was the impersonal hum of hospital monitoring equipment around her. At least, she consoled herself, she basically had her own private room since the other bed was unoccupied.

She shifted in agony, crunching the stiff scratchy linens, wincing at the pain in her muscles and joints. Everything ached. She tried to lay motionless on her hospital cot.

Even the roots of her hair hurt. She was constrained by the wires attached to her body monitoring her vital signs. She had to lie on her back, trapped as if she'd be captured by Lilliputians.

Careful not to detach the intravenous tubing in her arm, she gingerly reached for her head and felt the still painful bump.

The doctor had informed her earlier that she had a concussion, and was suffering, as well, from dehydration and shock. The doctor added she might have problems remembering things, but that she should just be thankful she didn't roll off that dungeon shelf into the pool of water rising from below.

She glanced up at a curtain, mounted in the ceiling, half drawn around her bed. It shielded her from the harsh hallway light coming in through the tiny window on the door to her room.

She needed to get rest, but her mind was cluttered with anxious thoughts of what had brought her to this hospital. She lay on her back and closed her eyes, listening to the rhythmic beeping sounds of hospital equipment.

In the darkness, a soft shaft of moonlight slipped through her window blinds, illuminating the bouquet of flowers Bjorn had purchased for Sarah earlier.

They never got to have dinner together that night. He rescued her instead.

She opened her eyes, remembering the comforting words of Mrs. Libris, who often engaged Sarah in conversation at Library.

She recalled one chat in particular.

Sarah was sharing her despair about how the Administrators once again had reduced her credits for teaching the truth.

Mrs. Libris responded by bringing out a book from her own personal collection. The little volume was titled "Philippians". It seemed to be a gentle list of advice about what to do when faced with distress.

Mrs. Libris had suggested that applying the meaning of these words to her own life would make Sarah feel a bit more optimistic about the future.

Sarah reasoned her current dismal situation warranted trying to remember the list, now that she was all alone in this dark antiseptic room.

She struggled to remember beginning with, "Focus on whatever is noble." That was all that came to her. "Not a very long list," she said to herself.

She smiled. Bjorn clearly proved himself noble by saving her life. Then she recalled the words 'friendly' and 'loveable'. Or was that 'lovely'? Well, that described Bjorn, too.

Then the rest of the words floated into her memory and tumbled from her lips, "Think about whatever is true, honorable, reverent, right, just, pure, modest, respectable, gracious, admirable, virtuous, and of moral excellence. This is what is truly worthwhile and worthy of praise."

There was nothing wrong with Sarah's brain. Concussion or not, she could remember that list from Mrs. Libris' little book. And, it did give her the feeling that the peace of God was with her.

She smiled, delighted, at the little plush toy attached to the bouquet of flowers.

Bjorn had asked a nurse for some scissors to trim down the thick rose and peony stems. Then, he had found a large disposable cup and filled it with ice chips, which started to melt into the pure water needed to keep the flowers alive.

Water. Very different from the turbulent dank swamp which nearly drowned her.

The flowers might die, but the feelings she felt for Bjorn grew stronger with each moment. That little plush toy was a gift, Bjorn told Sarah, from an appreciative shopkeeper who thanked Bjorn for being patient. She thought to herself that it was his patience which resulted in him rescuing her. He said he'd explain what actually had taken place at the castle, but only after she'd gotten some rest.

That little plush toy, tossed in to his purchase as an "Oh, by the way, thanks for your understanding", would now come to symbolize the night Bjorn saved Sarah's life.

She smiled, closed her eyes, and rested, whispering to herself, "Think on noble things, like the brave character of Bjorn Esterday."

Then, she heard her door creek open. The curtain obscured her view.

Struggling to sit up, Sarah called to the

unseen person, "Bjorn, you came back! I thought the hospital staff sent you..."

Sarah stopped.

"Bjorn?"

She didn't recognize the footsteps.

"Who is there? I can't see you. Please turn on the light."

But the lights remained off and nobody responded, yet the footsteps crept closer.

The hospital monitor, showed Sarah's heartbeat increased, her blood pressure went up, and her muscles tensed. She reached for the wireless nurse call button, but it clattered to the floor out of Sarah's reach.

Then, that person stepped into view for Sarah.

"Oh! You were the last person I was expecting to see..." Sarah exclaimed.

11 CHAPTER- What will happen next?

Skipper has asked to be locked into the dungeon. Bjorn refuses, but the foreman, who is tired of Skipper's constant changing demands, is all for locking up the fickle tyrant.

Bjorn wants to make a wonderful surprise dinner for Sarah at her place and after he buys the ingredients, he buys Sarah some flowers.

When he gets to her place, he sees a note and something clicks in Bjorn's memory.

He races back to the castle and with only the Foreman's help, tries to get there before it's too late... but where is "THERE"?

Will Bjorn find Sarah in time? What has happened to Skipper Courtly?

Skipper insists on being locked in the dungeon.

Bjorn is against it. The Foreman is all for it.

Bjorn wants Sarah to forget the distress of being unjustly fired from her job. He decides to buy ingredients for a dinner and pick up a bouquet of flowers.

When he gets to her place, there is a note waiting for him. He has missed Sarah's calls and realizes it may be too late. He rushes to the castle and enlists the foreman's help!

We see that the foreman and Bjorn rescue not just Sarah, but Skipper Courtly, as well.

And the thanks they get is that Skipper blames them for breaking the string on his violin. He doesn't even realize that his life was saved!

Skipper cannot comprehend that his life would never have been in danger if he were not so bent on trying to amass power.

Skipper does not accept that there never was any ghost.

Sarah is recovering in the hospital room and receives a mysterious visitor that she was not expecting at all!

&> To Be Continued... ⊗

12 Did You Know

What do you think about the concept of TRUST and how it differs from LOYALTY

Loyalty is making sure your team wants to stay with you to achieve the stated goal.
The formula for Loyalty is:

Team commitment + Lasting Relationships + Management supporting the team. This results in loyalty.

What would you do to inspire loyalty?
There are two cycles that need to occur before the team can trust the manager or the manager can trust the team workers.

First, the manager must prove to be competent in the skills needed to reach the goal. Each team member must also be competent in their individual skill set. The manager organizes those skills effectively.

Next, the manager must have a track record in consistently leading his team in delivering goals. That goes for the team members, as well. There is no tolerance for a team member who does not pull as effectively as the rest.

Third, the manager must show they are loyal to the goal and to the team members. The purpose of the team needs to be in alliance with the larger corporate goal. Then a genuine alliance of manager and team members occurs.

But, all parties must be open about all issues good and bad. Wins and failures.

They need to be aware of what is going on to plan their next steps. No sweeping hidden issues under the rug. This means everyone is accountable.

There is a final element in this formula.

Finally, a manager must have proven integrity. The team must know their manger's core beliefs will be consistent and upright. They want to know they are working for the good-guy. Managers expect the same from all team members. Team members need to share the same honorable level of ethics. You can't have somebody thinking stealing is wrong when another member thinks stealing is acceptable but getting caught is wrong.

A productive loyal team needs:
- Competence,
- Consistency,
- Loyalty and alliance of goals,
- Openness and accountability,
- Integrity and shared ethics from both managers and the team members

To keep an established process and just make sure it runs smoothly, you'll need homogeneity (homo-jen-AY-ity)

"...differences in functional background, education, or personality, are more often positively related to performance, for example in terms of creativity or group problem solving, but only when the group process is carefully controlled."

Trust is essential in all of this. The team must be able to TRUST the manager to speak the truth, and the team members must be trustworthy.

*(E.**Mannix**, M.A. **Neale** (2005) Diverse Teams in Organizations (PP. 43, Psychological Science in the Public Interest, Vol 6, No. 2)*

.

ABOUT Wynter Sommers

Wynter Sommers is the pseudonym for an American writing team, which harnesses multiple skills in technology, research, and education. Formally trained with a PhD in Education, Wynter Sommers blends academic classroom experience, with corporate sophistication, and a passion for developing more effective student insights.

Wynter Sommers has taught classrooms of enthusiastic children. She has a heart to inspire creativity and develop critical thinking skills, all to encourage students to make wise choices in life. She wants to impart the talent of honing one's skills in self-reliance and collaborative team work. Despite any environmental barriers outside of an individual's control, Wynter Sommers wishes to impart the message that genuine hope, love, and peace can help us overcome obstacles, and cement friendships. Wynter Sommers hopes you enjoy the other ***Bjorn Esterday Was not Born Yesterday*** stories in this series.

www.ingramcontent.com/pod-product-compliance
Lightning Source LLC
Chambersburg PA
CBHW051841020726
47502CB00005B/1905